Humphrey's Bedtime

Henry Holt and Company

New York

It was Baby's bedtime.
He had to go to bed first
because he was the smallest.

Humphrey's

Bedtime

To Georgia Lottie
Love Mum x

Henry Holt and Company, LLC
Publishers since 1866
115 West 18th Street
New York, New York 10011
www.henryholt.com

Henry Holt is a registered trademark of Henry Holt and Company, LLC.
Copyright © 2000 by Sally Hunter
All rights reserved.
First published in the United States in 2001 by Henry Holt and Company, LLC
Originally published in the United Kingdom in 2000 by Puffin Books

Library of Congress Catalog Card Number: 2001087763

ISBN 0-8050-6903-8 (hardcover)
3 5 7 9 10 8 6 4

ISBN 0-8050-7398-1 (paperback)
1 3 5 7 9 10 8 6 4 2

First published in hardcover in 2001 by Henry Holt and Company
First Owlet paperback edition—2003
Printed in Singapore

"Night, night."

"I am allowed to stay
up very, very late,"
said Lottie.

"That's because I am the biggest,

and that's what happens
when you are the biggest."

"Bathtime," called Mommy.

Humphrey made big bubble mountains

and magic potions.

He had a lovely time.

But when it was Lottie's
turn for her bath, she said,
"I don't have time for a bath.
My babies are soooo dirty.
They need a good wash."

And then she said,

"I don't go to bed yet.
I am a BIG GIRL."

"Nearly done, Bear."

"Jim-jams on."

"Suppertime," called Mommy.

Humphrey had hot milk
and buttery toast.

He felt warm and cozy in his tummy.

Mop liked his too.

But Lottie didn't want her supper.
She said,
"I don't have time for supper.
My babies keep complaining
they are hungry."

And then she said,

"I don't go to bed yet.
I am a BIG GIRL."

"Eat it all up and you will grow
big and strong."

"Neigh…neigh…up the wooden hill."

"Storytime," said Mommy.

It was Humphrey's favorite book.
He liked the pictures and the
magic fairies.

"Once upon a time,
there lived a little
pixie at the
bottom of the
garden..."

Humphrey was all snuggly...

and sleepy.

But Lottie didn't want her story.
She said,
"My babies are only little.
They are very tired.
I must tuck them up in bed."

And then she said,

"I don't go to bed yet.
I am a BIG GIRL."

But Lottie was having problems
with her babies.

Lulu was being silly,

Trevor wouldn't wear his
pajamas properly,

Barry wouldn't lie down,

and Bear had got lost.

Lottie felt all hot ...

...and CROSS!

"What's all this?" said Daddy.

"Come on, my funny little girl.

Off we go ...

...to...

...bed."